Rosie's Special Present

For our beautiful niece Rhiannon,
with love and kisses
M.M. and G.M.

ROSIE'S SPECIAL PRESENT
A JONATHAN CAPE BOOK 978 1 780 08037 6

Published in Great Britain by Jonathan Cape, an imprint of Random House Children's Publishers UK
A Penguin Random House Company

 Penguin
Random House
UK

This edition published 2015
1 3 5 7 9 10 8 6 4 2

Text copyright © Myfanwy Millward, 2015
Illustrations copyright © Gwen Millward, 2015

RANDOM HOUSE CHILDREN'S PUBLISHERS UK   61–63 Uxbridge Road, London W5 5SA

www.randomhousechildrens.co.uk   www.randomhouse.co.uk

Addresses for companies within The Random House Group Limited can be found at: www.randomhouse.co.uk/offices.htm

THE RANDOM HOUSE GROUP Limited Reg. No. 954009

A CIP catalogue record for this book is available from the British Library.

Printed in China

MIX
Paper from
responsible sources
FSC® C018179

Penguin Random House is committed to a sustainable future for our business, our readers and our planet.
This book is made from Forest Stewardship Council® certified paper.

Rosie's Special Present

For Rosie

Myfanwy Millward and Gwen Millward

JONATHAN CAPE | LONDON

Everyone was having tea when the present woke up.
"Where am I?" it thought.

Then it remembered: it was
Rosie's special present and
today was Rosie's special day.

The present wondered what Rosie was like.

Was she a princess
with a golden crown,

or a trapeze artist
in a circus,

or was she a pirate with
a squawking parrot?

For
Rosie

The present was worried.
It didn't like parrots.

It hoped Rosie was a princess living in a beautiful castle.

Then it imagined all the amazing presents a princess would have.

"What if all her presents look more exciting than me?" it thought. "I'll be forgotten about."

Rosie's present was so worried it decided to get out
of its box to see what the other presents were like.

It wasn't easy,
but it rolled

and jumped

and tumbled

and finally got out.

"Wow!" he gasped when he
saw all the balloons and ribbons.
"This **must** be a princess's castle!"

For Rosie

He didn't know that Rosie and her friends were eating
sandwiches and cake in the kitchen next door.
"When can I open my special present?" asked Rosie.
"When you've finished eating," said Rosie's mum.

Rosie was thinking about her present.
She was too excited to eat.

Rosie's present started looking at all the other gifts.
One had shiny paper with sparkling silver stars.
"That looks like a good present," he thought, tapping
it gently with his paw. "I wonder what's inside . . ."

Rosie's special present looked at all the glittering packages one by one . . .

but was happy that his own box with its giant gold bow, looked far more exciting than all the other gifts.

But then he had **another** thought.

"My box is so big and it has a such a giant bow that Rosie will think something really wonderful is inside . . .

like a magical bird . . .

or a juggling rabbit . . .

or a hundred dancing mice . . .

I have the best box, but when Rosie opens it,
will she think I'm the best present?"

Rosie's present swished his tail, feeling very worried.

He didn't know that Rosie couldn't wait to meet him. In the kitchen she was telling her friends all about her special present. "It's the best present in the world!" she said.

All the other children imagined what the best present in the world would look like.

Now Rosie's special
present was climbing
up the bookcase.
"If I wrap myself in
those colourful ribbons,
then I'll look more
exciting!" he thought.

But Rosie had **nearly**
finished her birthday
tea . . .

"Please, Mum, can I open my special present now?" asked Rosie.

"Wait until everyone's finished," said Mum.

Rosie's special present walked carefully along the top of the bookcase . . .

. . . and then he jumped,

until . . .

Now he **was** covered in colourful ribbons . . .
and bunting and balloons and flowers and wrapping paper!

Rosie ran into the room.

She didn't notice the big box with the giant gold bow.
She didn't notice the colourful ribbons.
She didn't even notice the mess.

All she noticed was her special present.

And he **was** the best present
she had ever had.

"Hello little kitten," said Rosie, giving him a giant hug. "I'm going to call you Max."

Rosie didn't look like a trapeze artist, or a pirate, or a princess. She looked like a friend, and she made Max feel **very** special.

Max felt so happy that he purred with joy.

It had been the best birthday ever, but it was just the beginning of a very special friendship for Rosie and Max . . .